Walt Disney's
The Ugly Dachshund

Senior Designer: Elaine Lopez
Editor: Sharon Fass Yates
Editorial Director: Pamela Pia

Walt Disney's The Ugly Dachshund copyright © 1973, 2006 Disney Enterprises, Inc.
Story adapted by Carl Memling from the motion picture "The Ugly Dachshund." Illustrations by Mel Crawford.

CE

Copyright ©2008 Disney Enterprises, Inc. All Rights Reserved.
Published by Reader's Digest Children's Books,
Reader's Digest Road, Pleasantville, NY U.S.A. 10570-7000
and Reader's Digest Children's Publishing Limited,
The Ice House, 124-126 Walcot Street, Bath UK BA1 5BG
Reader's Digest Children's Books, the Pegasus logo,
and Reader's Digest are all registered trademarks of
The Reader's Digest Association, Inc. Manufactured in China.
1 3 5 7 9 10 8 6 4 2

Walt Disney's
The Ugly Dachshund

Illustrated by The Walt Disney Studios

Illustrations by Mel Crawford

Story adapted by Carl Memling
from the motion picture "The Ugly Dachshund"

Reader's Digest
Children's Books™

Pleasantville, New York • Montréal, Québec • Bath, United Kingdom

Once there were three little Dachshund pups named Chloe, Heidi, and Wilhelma.

With them lived a fourth pup. His name was Brutus, and he was a Great Dane.

Poor Brutus. He thought he was a Dachshund, too, but a very large, clumsy, ugly one.

Brutus grew and he grew and he grew, as Great Dane pups always do. Soon, when Brutus stood on his hind legs, he was almost as tall as his owner, Mrs. Garrison.

One day Brutus jumped into a wheelbarrow to play with the "other" Dachshunds. *Crash!* The wheelbarrow was wrecked and the Dachshunds went flying in all directions.

"Oh no!" cried Mrs. Garrison.

Brutus kept on thinking that he was a
Dachshund. He even tried to run the way
Dachshunds do, low and close to the ground.
Chloe, Heidi, and Wilhelma pattered into
the house one day.

Chloe grabbed a ball of wool in her mouth and ran. Yipping and squealing, Heidi and Wilhelma chased after her. And big Brutus lumbered after them, trying to join in the fun.

The ball unwound and soon there was nothing but a tangled trail of wool.

The three Dachshunds scampered off. Before poor Brutus had a chance to follow them, in came Mrs. Garrison.

"Brutus!" she cried. "Look at what you've done!"

Then, another day, the three little Dachshunds and Brutus raced into Mr. Garrison's workroom.

The workroom was full of pencils and paints and brushes and paper.

Suddenly Brutus's tail knocked down a jar of paint brushes.

The big pup gave a yelp and backed into a cabinet.

Crash!

The cabinet toppled over—and paint tubes, pencils, and pads scattered all over the floor.

Then Brutus crashed into an enormous easel, just as the three little Dachshunds ran off.

"Oh no!" groaned Mr. Garrison as he rushed into the workroom. "Brutus! Look at what you've done!"

Poor Brutus whimpered sadly.

"Well, he's done it again," said Mrs. Garrison.

"Yes," said Mr. Garrison, "but after all, he's just a puppy."

"I know," sighed Mrs. Garrison. "That's what frightens me. What will he do when he gets bigger?"

Finally Mr. Garrison was forced to put Brutus outdoors in a pen.

After several mournful whimpers, the Great Dane pup settled down and closed his eyes.

Hours went by. All at once Brutus's eyes snapped open, and he growled. Rising, he began to paw at the sides of the pen.

In the darkness, a strange man was coming toward the house.

Brutus charged. In one big jump he
was out of the pen.

With a flying leap, he
knocked down the stranger—
and a gun flew through the air.

The stranger jumped to his feet and headed for a tree, with Brutus after him.

The man swung himself up into the tree just in time. Brutus circled below, barking loudly.

Inside the house, Mr. and Mrs. Garrison thought that Brutus was barking because he was lonely. They turned over and went back to sleep.

Poor Brutus.

In the morning, the strange man he had chased up the tree turned out to be a policeman looking for prowlers.

Mr. Garrison was sorry that the policeman had spent all night up in the tree. But he was delighted that Brutus was such a good watchdog.

So Brutus stayed on with the Garrisons and the Dachshunds.
"Really!" Mrs. Garrison wailed one day as Brutus tried to
snuggle into her lap. "We'll never have any peace until Brutus
stops thinking he's a Dachshund!"

By now Brutus was no longer an oversized pup. He was a *full grown* Great Dane, but he still thought he was a Dachshund.

Mr. Toyama, when he came to decorate the house for a party, thought something quite different. "Lion! Help! Lion!" he cried.

At the party that night, Mrs. Garrison proudly showed
Chloe to a friend.

"Isn't she a darling!" Mrs. Garrison said. "She never gets
into trouble the way Brutus does."

At that moment, in the backyard, Brutus was lunging with
all his strength against his leash. At last the knot gave way.

So Brutus was the next guest to arrive at the party. Barking his friendliest barks, he came galloping among the guests.

"Lion! Help! Lion!" Mr. Toyama cried.

Chairs splintered, tables toppled, and the guests scattered in all directions. The party was over.

Brutus was in disgrace. Even Mr. Garrison agreed that something would have to be done. But the next day Chloe fell into the garbage can. The garbage man came along and dumped all the litter and Chloe, too, into his truck. He was just about to drive off when—

"Wurf! Wurf!" Brutus barked and blocked his way.

Mr. and Mrs. Garrison came running out to scold him. But then they heard Chloe yipping faintly inside the truck.

"Gosh," said the garbage man when Chloe had been rescued, "I bet that's why Brutus wouldn't let me leave."

"It does look that way, doesn't it?" said Mrs. Garrison fondly.

Mrs. Garrison no longer complained about Brutus, but to her he was nothing more than a sweet, clumsy ox of a dog.

This troubled Mr. Garrison so much that then and there he decided to enter Brutus in the Fairview Dog Show.

Could Mr. Garrison train Brutus to be a show dog in so short a time? The Fairview Dog Show was only a few weeks away.

"Well, I can try," he told himself.

With the help of Doc Pruitt, a friendly kennel owner, he tried and tried. Brutus learned to heel and stay, but after many hours of hard work Doc Pruitt could only scratch his head in puzzlement.

"Why does he droop that way in the middle?" he asked.

"I'll tell you why," Mr. Garrison said gloomily. "He still thinks he's a Dachshund."

The day of the Fairview Dog Show arrived.

Mr. Garrison and Doc Pruitt led Brutus to a large tent.

His eyes wide and staring, Brutus saw for the first time: a Pekingese, a bulldog, a poodle, a bassett hound, and—

"Great Danes to the ring, please," called a judge.

Swallowing hard, Mr. Garrison led Brutus to the show ring.

And there Brutus—for the first time—saw other Great Danes!

How tall and strong they were! How handsome! What a proud, Great-Dane look they had about them!

Brutus eyed the other Danes.
Suddenly he lifted his head proudly.
At last he knew he was a Great Dane!
    Can you guess which Great Dane
won First Prize that day . . . ?

Brutus won!

As for Mrs. Garrison, she was both surprised and delighted. There are still three little Dachshunds living with the Garrisons. And with them lives a fourth dog of whom they're very proud. He is a huge and handsome Great Dane, and Brutus is his name.